'Guess what?' said Leotard. 'We've

'Move?' said Gruesome sitting u
beetle from her left ear. 'What d'you mean?'

'It's the council,' said Leotard. 'They're pulling down all the houses this side of Wellington Street to build a ring road. We'll all be rehoused in a multi-storey block.'

'But I don't want to be rehoused,' moaned Gruesome. 'I've just about got used to this place. At least it's got a back yard and water running down the walls in winter, even if the whole house is much too warm. But a multi-storey block . . . never.'

Jane Holiday

Gruesome and Bloodsocks Move House

Illustrated by Steven Appleby

Young Lions

First published in paperback in 1987 by Dragon Books
Reprinted 1987
Published in Young Lions 1988
Second impression September 1988

Young Lions is an imprint of
the Children's Division, part of
the Collins Publishing Group,
8 Grafton Street, London W1X 3LA

Printed and bound in Great Britain by
William Collins Sons & Co. Ltd, Glasgow

To
Susan and Terry Dicken,
in whose Museum Café, St Ives,
I wrote this book

1

It was early summer.

Augusta Vampire (otherwise known as Gruesome Gussie) was lying in her back yard. She was sucking her favourite spinach-flavoured ice-lolly. Bloodsocks, her cat, (so-called because his paws were the colour of dried blood) was sitting on top of the dustbin moodily munching a fresh earthworm. They had lived in Trumpington now for nearly a year but Gruesome was still not quite used to living in a house. It wasn't so bad in the winter when damp patches and fungi appeared on the ceilings and the wind whistled through the cracks in the doors and made the windows rattle in their frames. But in summer, even with all the doors and windows open, it was hard to bear.

'Hiya Grue,' came a voice.

It was Leotard Jones from next door. He was peering over from the ginnel into the back yard.

When Gruesome had first met Leotard, his head had been shaved and there had been a smiling face painted on it. Now he had let his hair grow again and it was long enough to tie back in a small pigtail.

'Guess what?' he said, as he climbed over Gruesome's rickety back gate. 'We've all got to move.'

'Move?' said Gruesome sitting up and removing a small beetle from her left ear. 'What d'you mean?'

'It's the council,' said Leotard. 'They're pulling down all the houses this side of Wellington Street. They're going to build a ring road. We'll all be re-housed.'

'I don't want to be re-housed,' said Gruesome. 'This house is bad enough – the next one might be worse.'

'Mum's dead chuffed,' Leotard said. 'We're going to have a flat on the ground floor in a multi-storey block. It's got central heating.'

Gruesome moaned and Bloodsocks wobbled down the drainpipe (he had become disgustingly fat during the last year) and began to knead Gruesome's bony legs reassuringly.

'I said you wouldn't like it but Mum wouldn't listen,' Leotard said, tickling one of Bloodsocks' many chins.

'Like it?' said Gruesome. 'Like it? I've just about got used to this place. At least it's got a back yard and water running down the walls in winter. The bathroom's OK too even if the whole house is much too warm. But a multi-storey block . . . never.'

'Cool it,' said Leotard. 'Let's have a drink, eh? As our Ron says, it may never happen.'

Gruesome went inside. 'Here,' she said, returning with a tray containing two chipped mugs and a saucepan lid of cake. 'Try this – it's a garlic milkshake.'

'Wicked,' said Leotard, gulping it down at great speed. 'What's the cake then?'

'Parsnip with strawberry icing,' said Gruesome.

Leotard ate three slices. Bloodsocks had one slice while Gruesome didn't even have a sip of tea.

'Multi-storey block,' she muttered, watching absentmindedly as Bloodsocks licked the icing off his whiskers. 'Central heating. I'd be better off in Dieppe with Uncle Batticoop, Four-Fanged Francis, Hideous Hattie, Hirudinea and Annelid.'

'Go on,' said Leotard. 'You've forgotten what they're like.'

A sudden vision of Uncle Batticoop saying, 'Metamorphose, Augusta' came into Gruesome's mind. She remembered the vampires' nightly blood-hunting expeditions. Most of all she remembered the loathsome smell of fresh blood and how she was sick if she even attempted to drink any and came out in silver spots. She remembered too the vicious nips Four-Fanged Francis (who had then been Five-Fanged Francis) had given her on many occasions and the way the other vampires used to sneer at her. And perhaps, worst of all, was the memory of Uncle Batticoop's lo——ng lectures on the duties of a vampire, how they came from a respectable line of Transylvanian vampires and so on and so forth and so fifth.

'You're right,' she said. 'They were awful. I don't want to go to Dieppe.'

Just as she said these words there was a sudden screeching and hissing from what sounded like a gigantic bellows and a huge dark shape plummeted down, coming to rest among the rosebay willowherb and dandelions. It looked like a bundle of rags.

Bloodsocks leapt up in alarm, his back arched, claws extended. Gruesome and Leotard watched in amazement as the bundle of rags flapped and staggered to its feet, shaping itself into a bird with a long bare neck and beaky head.

It was Hideous Hattie's pet vulture Wuneye.

2

'Wuneye,' cried Gruesome in amazement. 'Whatever are you doing in Trumpington?' (Not that it was any good asking him – all he ever did was caw horribly and fly about in a dispirited and ungainly manner). Wuneye had always been a raggy-looking bird but now he looked terrible.

'I wonder what's happened,' said Gruesome. 'I hope it doesn't mean trouble. If Wuneye comes, can Hideous Hattie be far behind?'

'Caaaaaaaaaaaaawwwwwwwwwwwwwww,' said Wuneye, and flopped back on to the ground, exhausted.

Gruesome looked at him closely. His feathers had always looked a bit raggy as if he was slowly being eaten by moths, but now he looked worse than ever. His one bloodshot eye (the left) was half-closed and he had a lump on the back of his head. His talons were encrusted with mud.

'Here, give me a hand with this bird,' Gruesome said firmly to Leotard. 'What he needs is a good bath.'

She gripped Wuneye at the back of his scrawny neck and Leotard took firm hold of his tail feathers.

In a few minutes a violently protesting vulture was dumped in the bath (which now had a splendid variety of plants, algae and tadpoles in addition to Marcus) and hosed down with cold water.

'Now don't try and bite me or Leotard,' Gruesome said firmly to Wuneye as she dumped him on top of an unwary tadpole. 'And *don't* scratch. If you do, we'll put the plug in and just let you drown.'

Wuneye fluttered his one mouldy eyelid which Gruesome took to be a sign of agreement. When she and Leotard had washed him thoroughly the bath was crawling with fleas, ticks and bugs and the plants were the colour of sludge. Wuneye himself looked considerably smaller. They carried

10

him downstairs and Leotard dried him with a hairdryer borrowed from his Mum.

As soon as he was dry, Wuneye fled out of the window and down Wellington Street.

'Not a pretty sight,' said Leotard, watching the vulture's somewhat drunken flight over the housetops.

Gruesome was worried. She'd forgotten all about the council threatening to move her into a multi-storey block. There were more urgent things to worry about. Where were Hideous Hattie and the rest of them? Was she to have no peace?

She took the mugs and saucepan lid back inside. 'Watch out for Wriggoletto,' she called to Leotard. 'She loves trying to trip visitors up.'

Wriggoletto was a newcomer to Gruesome's house. She was a grass snake who was adept at coiling herself up into a tight spring and then unwinding herself very fast. She loved slithering out in front of people and making them trip over. She'd done it to Big Pete, the gravedigger, and Mr Todd, the butcher.

11

Wriggoletto didn't try to trip up Leotard though. Last time she'd tried, he'd just trodden on her and bruised her tail. She just wound herself round his left ankle and unzipped the pocket on the leg of his jeans and snuffled inside.

Crash Crash Crash.

Gruesome rushed to the front door.

Mrs Musa from down the road stood on the doorstep looking very angry indeed. She was brandishing a rolling-pin. She was a tall woman with wet-permed hair and she wore a pink T-shirt and shorts and white plastic sandals.

'There ought to be a law against them,' she shouted when she saw Gruesome.

Gruesome stared at her in surprise. Had Bloodsocks got up to something? No, there he was, rubbing himself round Mrs Musa's ankles. He thought everyone was his friend.

Mrs Musa stormed past her, along the passage through to the kitchen and out through the back door. Fortunately Wriggoletto was still in Leotard's trouser leg pocket so she was unable to trip Mrs Musa up.

Mrs Musa stood in the back yard, casting a look of distaste

at the rambling abandon of weeds and bones, before looking up at the drainpipe.

'There,' she said, shaking her rolling-pin. 'Just look at that – and my Sam home in half an hour for his lunch.'

On top of the drainpipe crouched Wuneye. Held between his now-gleaming talons was a large juicy-looking steak. He ripped big lumps out of it with his curved beak and appeared to swallow them whole. A trickle of blood oozed from his jaws. The lump on the back of his head bobbed up and down like a misplaced Adam's apple.

'Give him heartburn, I shouldn't wonder,' said Gruesome.

Mrs Musa burst into tears. 'Burst in bold as a bazooka and stole it off my kitchen-table,' she said. 'Enough to give anyone the jittering jellybabies for a week. What are you going to do about it then? My Sam'll be home in a minute, hungry as ten tigers.'

3

Gruesome managed to pacify Mrs Musa by buying her an even larger piece of steak than the one Wuneye had stolen. Then she had to tell the whole story to Mrs Jones (Leotard's Mum) who wanted to know what all the fuss was about.

'I hope them other lot aren't coming back,' Mrs Jones said. 'Didn't reckon much to them – no offence like,' she said, catching sight of Gruesome's highly-polished, whiter-than-white fangs, 'but I know you were never right fond of them.'

At last Gruesome was left alone and was able to lie down in her coffin for a little rest. The sight of the blood had made her feel faint. In fact a silver spot had appeared on the tip of her nose just from the smell of it. She lay down with the reassuring weight of Bloodsocks on her stomach. Wriggoletto snuggled herself round her head.

'Stinking hellebore,' she muttered as there was another bang at the door. 'Can't one even sleep quietly in one's coffin?'

She squashed Bloodsocks under one arm and shuffled off to the door once again.

A policeman stood there.

'Are you Miss Augusta Vampire, otherwise known as Gruesome Gussie?' he asked, gazing nervously at Wriggoletto who was slowly uncoiling herself from Gruesome's head and obviously preparing to re-attach herself elsewhere.

'That's right,' said Gruesome. 'Do come in.'

It wasn't any of the policemen she knew. She'd become acquainted with PC Beard and PC Gartside when Bloodsocks (and some other animals) had been kidnapped the year before. This policeman was black with very broad shoulders and a neat moustache. He spoke briefly into his

walkie-talkie set and then followed Gruesome into the front room.

'*Booooiiiiiiiiinnnnnnnggggggg,*' went the sofa as it usually did when it was sat upon.

Bloodsocks leapt on to the policeman's knee and began to purr. The policeman visibly sagged under this unexpected weight. (A year of easy living and good food had not improved Bloodsocks' appearance.)

'I'm PC Williams,' he said. 'I've had a complaint.' He put his helmet down beside him on the sofa. 'It's in regard to a bird allegedly residing at this address.'

'Bird?' said Gruesome. 'There's no bird living here. Just me and Bloodsocks,' (she pointed to the cat busily pulling threads in PC William's trousers). 'And . . . er . . . Wriggo-letto . . .' She pointed to the snake now happily asleep inside the helmet. 'And of course Marcus and . . . er . . . his family.'

'Marcus?' asked PC Williams.

'A frog,' said Gruesome, disappearing into the kitchen as she remembered she hadn't offered him a drink.

She returned with a glass of parsnip juice and some nettle tarts.

'So there is definitely no bird (species vulture) residing

here then, Miss . . . er . . . Vampire? According to information received,' PC Williams said, consulting his notepad, 'a vulture was seen at 11.45 A.M. in your back yard.'

That Mrs Musa, thought Gruesome, after all the money I spent buying her an even juicier steak than the one Wuneye ate.

'No bird lives at this address, officer,' Gruesome said firmly.

'Well, I'll just take a look out there if you don't mind, Miss. Have to follow through these reports, you know.'

Gruesome pulled Bloodsocks off his lap and PC Williams dusted his trousers now littered with black hairs and followed her out.

Now for it, thought Gruesome. Whatever shall I do? She made as much noise as possible in the kitchen, hoping to warn Wuneye, although she knew he would probably be fast asleep after his meal and his exhausting flight.

'You see,' she said triumphantly, looking in great relief at the now unoccupied drainpipe. 'No birds here, officer.' She sniffed and tapped her fangs.

PC Williams twitched nervously. He looked all round the back yard. Leotard was sitting on the dustbin painting his fingernails a bright green. He took no notice of PC Williams.

'My neighbour's son, Leotard Jones,' said Gruesome.

'Been here long, have you?' asked the policeman.

'All morning,' said Leotard, pausing in his work to admire his left hand.

'Seen any vultures, have you?' asked PC Williams desperately.

'You what?' said Leotard, looking at PC Williams for the first time. 'Where d'you think this is then? Knowsley Safari Park or summat?'

'I'll be off then,' said the policeman to Gruesome. 'Looks like a false alarm.' Gruesome followed him back inside turning to look at Leotard who gave her a big wink.

'*Aaaaaaaaaaaaaaaaaaaaah*'

Gruesome rushed in to find the policeman had jammed

his helmet on his head with Wriggoletto clinging frantically to his right ear. As soon as Gruesome had uncoiled her, PC Williams tore out of the house and shot off down the road in his 'panda', leaving his helmet behind.

'A policeman's lot is not a happy one, Bloodsocks,' said Gruesome as she left the helmet by the front door in case he came back for it.

4

As soon as the 'panda' was safely out of sight, Gruesome
went out to the back yard again. Leotard grinned and got
off the dustbin. He removed the lid with a flourish.

'Hey presto,' he said. Inside lay Wuneye fast asleep, with
two talons stuck in his mouth like a baby sucking a dummy.
'I shoved him in there as soon as I looked out of my
bedroom window and saw the 'panda' coming.' (The Joneses
lived in the flat above Gruesome in the terraced council
house). 'A good thing he didn't wake up and try and escape.'

'You'd better leave the lid off,' said Gruesome. 'I don't
want him to suffocate, horrible though he is.'

For the next few days Gruesome had a worrying time.
First she had to feed Wuneye and keep him hidden, or she
would get into trouble from the police. Then also she had to
keep a lookout for the vampires, whom she felt sure would
turn up at any moment now that Wuneye was back in town.
The worst part was getting food for the vulture without

arousing suspicion. It was well-known in Trumpington that she loathed blood and indeed meat of any kind, so she had to send Leotard instead. He couldn't always get away to feed Wuneye so she had to do it. The meat was very expensive and Gruesome found she was using all her dole money on feeding the vulture so that she couldn't afford to buy Bloodsocks any *Pussiesteaks*. (They had now used up the year's supply of *Pussiesteaks* which had been given to them by the manager of the Kwikbuy supermarket.) Bloodsocks had become quite unaccustomed to catching mice or fending for himself in any way and began to sulk when Gruesome offered fish fingers and fricassee of dandelion. He had come to expect fresh cream and cod boiled in milk whenever *Pussiesteaks* were not forthcoming and did not take at all kindly to their sudden withdrawal.

Perhaps the worst part was trying to keep Wuneye out of the way until he had eaten and forcing him to eat indoors instead of on top of the roof or drainpipe.

'It's no good, Grue,' said Leotard one day. 'You'll have to send someone else for the meat today. Mr Todd's getting right suspicious. He knows we don't usually eat all that steak – we usually buy steak about once a week and then we have sausages and pies. I have to keep offering to do all the shopping, so my mum won't go in there in case he says summat to her.'

Worst of all, one morning Gruesome woke up and found she was covered head to toe in silver spots. Spots on her face and neck, spots on her hands and arms, spots on her legs and feet and spots all over her body. She even had spots on her fangs.

Gruesome felt very conspicuous as she went out shopping in her usual long dress and canvas shoes. She felt that everyone was staring at her.

Mrs Thomas was scrubbing her doorstep as usual when Gruesome went past. Susie, her Scottie, was sitting nearby.

She took one look at Gruesome and ordered Susie in.

'Don't want her to catch measles,' she explained. 'She's very delicate – never been the same since the kidnapping.'

'I haven't got measles,' began Gruesome but Mrs Thomas wasn't listening.

'You ought to watch out for Bloodsocks too,' she said. 'He might catch it. Looks more like a pony these days than a cat.'

Indeed Bloodsocks' neck had become so fat that Gruesome had thrown his cat-collar away and bought one intended for dogs. She could still hear Mrs Thomas laughing when they reached the bottom of Wellington Street. She looked at Bloodsocks appraisingly.

'You *are* enormous, Bloodsocks,' she said. 'I think you ought to go on a diet. You don't want to get a heart-attack.'

Bloodsocks was annoyed. First he was deprived of his *Pussiesteaks*, boiled cod and cream, now he was told he was too fat. He thought Gruesome looked like a walking coat-hanger, but so what? She was his Gruesome, provider of all his comforts, and he loved her. He could run circles round that stupid little Susie, and Wriggoletto too, if he chose. He stalked on ahead, straining at his lead to annoy Gruesome.

Gruesome did her shopping as quickly as possible and rushed home to find Mrs Jones waiting for her. So of course Gruesome had to invite her in. Mrs Jones had become used to the black dustbin liners at the windows, the milk bottles full of decayed flowers and the collage of a rattle of skeletons on the wall and took no notice.

'Guess what Gruesome?' she said as she sat down. (*Boooiiiiiiiiinnnnnnnnngggggg*.) 'The council's re-housing us in two weeks. Two *weeks*. Just imagine. Don't give you much time do they? I expect – hey,' she broke off. 'What's up? You're all covered in spots. It's not catching is it? I don't want our Leotard getting it. It were bad enough when he had measles, chicken-pox and whooping-cough.' She got to her feet.

'No, no. It's just an allergy,' said Gruesome.

'Oh,' said Mrs Jones in relief. 'You're allergic. Our Bet's allergic. As soon as she even smells a jellied eel, her nose blows up like a balloon. Horrible it is.'

Gruesome wished Jean Jones would go away and leave her in peace.

'Well, I'll see you, love. Look after yourself.' She looked vaguely at the up-turned police-helmet by the front door. 'I see you've bought a flowerpot. Look lovely with one of them climbing plants. You could train it round your front door. Still, no point now, eh? We've been condemned. Cheerio love. Hope you'll soon be feeling better. Tara. Hey – here's your post. That's the same envelope we had . . . must be the letter from the council.' She waited for Gruesome to open it.

It was.

'Dear Miss Vandal,' (*Why do people always get my name wrong*? thought Gruesome crossly.)

'We are happy to inform you that we have at last found alternative accommodation for you. As you know, all the council property in Wellington is under a compulsory purchase order and is to be demolished some time this year to make way for a ring-road.

You have been allocated a one-bedroom, centrally-heated flat on the twentieth floor of the newly-built block just outside Trumpington. Your new address will be 20a Lilliputian Mansions, Windy Corner, Near Trumpington. You are welcome to

inspect your future home at any time between 10 and 11 A.M. Monday to Friday, subject to confirmation with the Council.

I remain,

Your obedient servant,

Hermione Grubb

(Housing Manager).'

'There you are,' said Mrs Jones. 'Same block as us only we're on the ground floor on account of our Leotard. Tara. See you love.'

Gruesome returned miserably after this depressing news to find Bloodsocks playing tag with Wriggoletto and Marcus while Wuneye was flying desperately around the room with a wastepaper basket stuck to his head.

'Oh death, where is thy sting? Oh grave, where is thy victory?' muttered Gruesome wearily as she clamped Wuneye between her knees and attempted to free him.

5

Deliverance was at hand the next day however. First of all Gruesome refused to feed Wuneye any more meat. 'You can have fish fingers or soya burgers,' she said. 'Otherwise starve.'

Wuneye wasn't in a position to argue. He hunched on top of the wardrobe and moodily crunched up a thirty pack of fish fingers and a few dog biscuits Gruesome had thrown in for good measure.

Bloodsocks had decided, after an exceedingly exhausting game of tag, that he did need more exercise and was swinging on the door frame.

'Hey Grue,' came a voice from the back. Leotard swung over the wall and let himself into the kitchen. 'Guess what?' he said, watching Gruesome stir a few woodlice into the omelette she was preparing.

'What?' asked Gruesome wearily.

'My mum wants me to visit Auntie Pat in London while

she's getting ready to move. Says I'll only get under her feet.'

'Oh,' said Gruesome. She was tired through not having sufficient time to worry properly about all her problems.

'Yes,' said Leotard, 'and Dad says he reckons you should go down with me. He thinks you might find a better place to live there – even a job. He says, if you pack up all your gear, he knows a chap going down with a part load of furniture and he can take yours free, if there isn't too much. Just take the most important things. That's if you want to go of course.'

'Yes,' cried Gruesome. 'Anything rather than live in a multi-storey block. What should I take then?'

'Bed, table, sofa, chairs and such,' said Leotard. 'We can always store it in someone's garage or garden. And all your clothes and stuff.'

'I haven't got a bed,' said Gruesome. 'I sleep in a coffin.'

'Sure,' said Leotard. 'Same difference. My dad says he'll pay for your train ticket because you'll be keeping an eye on me.'

Gruesome began to cheer up. 'Wonderful,' she said. 'Then even if Uncle Batticoop, Hideous Hattie, Four-Fanged Francis, Annelid and Hirudinea do come back, I won't be here.'

'Right,' said Leotard. 'And if you find a good place – you can stay with our Auntie Pat to start with – you can just stay in London and they'll never find out where you are. Your spots are going down a bit but you still look very green.'

'But what about Wuneye?' asked Gruesome. 'I'm not taking him.'

'Don't worry about him,' said Leotard. 'He'll just have to learn to look after himself.'

'I suppose so,' said Gruesome, 'but he's a real wally. I don't want him to get into any trouble.'

Gruesome felt happier than at any time since she had seen the five vampires off to Dieppe.

'I wonder if I have to buy a ticket for Bloodsocks,' she

wondered. 'And what about Wriggoletto and Marcus? Will they want to come, I wonder?'

She went into the undertaker's to pay off the last instalment on the HP for her coffin.

'Proving hardwearing I hope?' Mr Jackson enquired politely.

'Fine,' said Gruesome. 'Gives a good night's sleep.'

'Good, good. Well, they're built to last of course. Thank you. Always glad of your custom.'

'I don't think I'll need your services again,' said Gruesome. 'That coffin should last me a lifetime.'

Leotard came round later on to tell her that Den, an old friend of his dad, would take all her gear except the coffin.

'He's a bit superwhatsit, my dad says. He won't take nail or splinter of it. But not to worry. It can go in the guard's van on the train.'

'Great,' said Gruesome who was just going out to buy a cat basket.

'Don't forget to bring some butties and something to drink,' said Leotard. 'All they sell on trains, my mum says, is cardboard sandwiches and cups of dishwater, and not even that usually.'

'OK,' said Gruesome, and it was decided that they should take the 9.41 train the following Wednesday morning arriving at King's Cross Station at 12.50.

But a disturbing thing happened before Gruesome left. She woke up the next morning to find Wuneye had disappeared.

6

The next day Mr Jones' friend, Den, came with his removal van and loaded on to it the sofa, chairs, table, bean bags and TV set, all the old furniture that Big Pete had brought her when she first moved into the council flat. It wasn't much but Gruesome thought it might come in useful if she and Bloodsocks ever found a place of their own in London.

'Don't know for sure when I'll be going down love,' said Den, 'but here's my phone number in London so you can get in touch. See you, doll.'

All the furniture she had now was her coffin. She'd bought an old suitcase from a jumble sale and she packed her collage, snakeskins and her small collection of clothes. She had bought a dog basket . . . for Bloodsocks. None of the cat baskets was large enough.

Gruesome took it home, shut it and told Bloodsocks to keep away from it. Of course Bloodsocks immediately climbed into it, sniffed it thoroughly and fell asleep.

Gruesome spent the rest of the day preparing a special mushroom and custard paté for sandwiches as well as baking some nettle tartlets.

She tucked herself into her coffin that night quite excited. Mr Todd had promised to drive her, Leotard and Leotard's mum to the railway station in the morning in plenty of time for the train. If Wuneye had escaped, well, it wasn't her fault. He'd just have to take the consequences and be put into quarantine. She slept peacefully in her coffin with Bloodsocks' massive bulk curled up on her stomach and Wriggoletto coiled round her left foot.

In the morning Gruesome had a quick breakfast, took the sandwiches and drinks for the journey out of the fridge (Big Pete had promised to sell the cooker and fridge for her and send the money on), cunningly caught Bloodsocks unawares

and shut him into the basket, tied a piece of rope round the suitcase which kept bursting open, and said farewell to the Hairiettas, the spider's many daughters, who had established themselves in cobwebs up and down the house.

Marcus leapt into the frog basket made for him by Leotard.

'Where on earth's Wriggoletto?' asked Gruesome as Leotard came to collect her. His hair was now long enough to wear in a plait on one side and he had a silver hoop earring in one ear. A red square was painted on his right cheek, a blue moon on the left cheek and a yellow star on his forehead. He wore dark blue cotton trousers with turnups, a white T-shirt saying 'COOL', yellow braces, an oversized jacket and canvas boots.

'I like your face,' Gruesome said, who had never seen him looking so smart.

'I'll do yours for you if you like when we get on the train. Our Ron did mine. He's given me some paints to do it with.'

A car horn sounded outside.

'We'd better hurry. That's Mr Todd,' said Gruesome. 'If only I could find Wriggoletto . . .'

'She's probably in the suitcase,' said Leotard.

'But she'll suffocate,' Gruesome wailed.

'Go on. That suitcase is more holes than anything. You'd have to try to suffocate in that.'

Toot . . . Toot.

Gruesome took a last look round, picked up the suitcase and the dog box and handed a carrier bag and the frog basket to Leotard and slammed the door. Someone had filled the helmet up with earth, she noticed.

Outside Mr and Mrs Jones were loading Leotard's suitcase into the boot of Mr Todd's car. Mr Jones turned to look at his son with disapproval.

'Ee, what have you done now? Always up to some nonsense. Bet it was that pillock our Ron put you up to it.'

'It's *his* face,' said Mrs Jones. 'Anyway, he's going down to London – I dare say he won't be noticed there.'

'His Aunt Pat'll notice,' grunted Mr Jones. 'Shouldn't be surprised if she took a scrubbing-brush to him. Serve him right too.' Leotard looked completely untroubled by this prediction, Gruesome noticed.

At Trumpington station, several people had come to see Gruesome and Leotard off. There was Big Pete in boiler suit and boots as usual. He had been Gruesome's first friend in Trumpington and had helped her furnish her flat. He gave her a great hug and pressed a large pork pie into her hands.

'Keep you going like, while you're in London,' he said, as if Gruesome would have nothing else to eat until she returned to Trumpington.

'I don't know if I'll be coming back,' she said.

'You'll be back,' said Big Pete. 'You'll be back right enough.'

Mr Todd gave them a big bottle of Dandelion and Burdock to drink on the train. Mrs Thomas (and Susie) and the Patel twins had come to see them off as well so there was quite a crowd of them.

'Take care of yourself now, Leotard,' said Mrs Jones. 'Don't get up to anything daft.'

'Don't get up to anything daft,' snorted her husband. 'It's

our Leotard you're talking about, you know. Telling him not to be daft is like telling Rice Krispies not to snap, crackle and pop.'

At last all the doors on the train had been slammed shut and the guard was just raising the whistle to his lips when a commotion broke out at the ticket barrier.

'Stop! Stop!' came a loud voice. 'Stop that bird. Come back Sir. Come back Madam.' A steaming of porters, guards, ticket-collectors and inspectors rushed on to the platform.

Five figures, all too familiar to Gruesome, seemed to appear from nowhere. It was Uncle Batticoop, Hideous Hattie, Four-Fanged Francis, Annelid and Hirudinea.

The bird was, of course, Wuneye.

7

Wuneye made a swoop for an open carriage window, banged his head on the side and just managed to lurch through, flopping on to the feet of a middle-aged man with a grey beard.

Meanwhile the five vampires were battling wildly with the combined staff of Trumpington Railway Station.

'They should be asleep at this time of day,' said Gruesome, peering out of the window. 'They must have had a special blood-injection to keep them awake. But why aren't they in Dieppe?'

Meanwhile the man with the grey beard had removed Wuneye from his feet and had descended from the train to place the (now) unconscious bird on the platform.

Hideous Hattie wrested herself from the clasp of a BR ticket-collector and dashed towards him.

'Murderers, Muggers, Vandals.' She stopped to think of something really insulting and came out with, 'You HUMAN. Look what you've done to a poor defenceless vulture with six starving babes to feed.'

It was news to Gruesome that Wuneye had six starving babes to feed. If he'd ever had any progeny, she felt he would probably have abandoned them on a rock or thrown them to the wolves.

Uncle Batticoop had managed to get the better of the railway guard by knocking the guard's hat over his eyes and stealing his whistle while Four-Fanged Francis and Hirudinea had knocked over the remaining staff and were sitting on them.

All the passengers were peering out of doors and windows in amazement and delight. They liked a good show in Trumpington and this was certainly a good 'un.

Uncle Batticoop looked up and saw Gruesome staring at him in horror. He pointed a green and knotty finger at her.

33

He'd got a new top hat, Gruesome noticed, but otherwise looked just as dingy and decayed and unpleasant as he always had done. Hideous Hattie, Annelid and Hirudinea signalled their disgust by sitting on the ground while Four-Fanged Francis hissed.

'You wretched ungrateful creature,' Uncle Batticoop yelled at Gruesome. 'Yes . . . you, Augusta. You're the one I mean. How dare you harry and harass poor Wuneye? After all we've done for you. I always knew no good would come of you, ever since you drank that Coca-Cola.'

'Drank that Coca-Cola,' piped up Four-Fanged Francis advancing towards Gruesome, obviously prepared to give her an extra special nip to make up for all the nips she'd missed since he'd been in Dieppe. That was his mistake. The other ticket-collector, whom he'd been sitting on, leaped up and tackled Uncle Batticoop (who was just crunching up a dead wasp), while Leotard brought his new cricket-bat down on Four-Fanged Francis' head. There was a loud crunch.

'*Eeeeeeeeeeeeeeeekkkkkkkkkkkkkkkk. Aaaaaaarrrrgggg-hhhhhhhhh*,' shrieked Four-Fanged Francis, waving his arms like a berserk windmill. He looked with horror at a long, curved blackish-green object lying on the platform.

'You're THREE-FANGED Francis now,' shouted Gruesome amid loud wailings and screamings from all the other vampires, who had now been successfully recaptured.

'Quick!' shouted the guard. 'Let's get this train off before we have any more trouble. We'll see to this lot afterwards.' Even as he spoke, a 'panda' car drew up with a screeching siren and out leapt PC Williams. The guard felt in his pocket.

'Drat it. Here Fred, lend me your whistle.'

But Fred too had lost his whistle in the scrimmage. Eventually Leotard leant as far as he could out of the train window and as the guard dropped his red flag, Leotard stuck his fingers in his mouth and gave them one of his football specials. As the train departed they could still hear the siren on the 'panda' car screaming away. 'It must have got jammed,' said Leotard as they all settled comfortably into their seats.

8

The train journey, Gruesome felt, was rather dull. She wondered fleetingly what had made the other vampires return from Dieppe and whether they would be put in prison for assault. Then she forgot about them.

Bloodsocks let out a few bloodcurdling howls which Gruesome tried to ignore, fearing he would be a nuisance if he was let out.

'Let the poor thing out, dear,' said a woman in pink dungarees sitting at the opposite window. 'You've got a spare seat beside you.'

'S'right,' said Leotard. 'You can put him on the lead.'

Everyone looked rather shocked when they saw it was a cat. 'Stone me,' said a man with a ginger beard. 'Call that a cat? I've seen smaller pandas.'

Leotard passed the time painting Gruesome's face. He chose a sickly yellow and a bright pink to contrast with her pale greeny-pink skin (at the moment still faintly speckled with silver spots). He even painted her fangs emerald green.

'Hey, you look something else, Grue,' he said. 'If I didn't know you, I'd be frit stiff.'

Marcus amused himself by jumping out of the frog basket into the luggage-rack above and back again, to the entertainment of numerous children who seemed to appear like magic as soon as he started. Soon the entire gangway was blocked in both directions and no one could get to the toilets or to the buffet car.

'Pack it in, Marcus,' said Leotard. 'You're causing a traffic jam.'

Thwarted, the children diverted their attention to Bloodsocks who of course revelled in their attention and ate up smoky bacon crisps, half-eaten sardine sandwiches, bits of

squashed swiss roll oozing jam and buttercream and diges-
tive biscuits non-stop.

'I just hope he's not going to be sick,' Gruesome said to
Leotard. 'Honestly that cat hasn't the discrimination of a
louse. Stuffs himself with carbohydrates, salt and animal fat
and then he'll expect me to give him the kiss of life when he
gets a heart attack.'

Bloodsocks ignored this remark and licked a few spots of
cream off the seat.

At last the children were put to flight by the ticket-
collector who blenched at the sight of Gruesome, scowled at
Leotard and muttered darkly when he saw Bloodsocks about
cats travelling free not taking up places meant for humans.
Bloodsocks however, rubbed against his arm and mewed
and purred so coyly that he at last produced half a shortcake
biscuit for him from his pocket.

Just as everyone was quietly dozing, there was a loud
scream from a compartment lower down the train.

'What a noise,' said Gruesome. 'Those children again, I
suppose,' and settled back to sleep.

In the next compartment but one, the ticket-collector,

stretching his hand out to punch a ticket inspired screams in the passengers.

Round the length of his arm, from shoulder to wrist, coiled a snake.

Wriggoletto *had* been in the suitcase.

9

As the news spread to all compartments that there was a dangerous python/boa-constrictor/raccoon/man-eating tiger at large, the more fearful passengers scrambled on to the tables and stood on the seats. Babies and toddlers were stowed in the luggage racks. As soon as Gruesome heard the word 'snake' she knew what had happened. She rushed through the carriages until she came upon the unfortunate ticket-collector who had fainted into the arms of a very fat man carrying six bags of crisps and two British Rail ham sandwiches, while a schoolboy, who had taken a first-aid course at evening class and was dying to try it out, was giving him the kiss of life. Wriggoletto meanwhile had slithered away and cunningly coiled herself round the emergency cord just below the notice saying '£50 fine for improper use', thus preventing an entire family from eating and drinking.

Gruesome appeared, prised Wriggoletto off and re-coiled her round her greenish-black hair which Leotard had lacquered into stiff tussocks around her head.

The youngest child, a small girl with short fair hair, immediately grabbed an apple out of the basket and began to chew.

'Look Mum. It's Gravella and the Ghouls,' one of the children cried, looking at Gruesome's painted face, long, rather dusty flowered dress and black jelly shoes. 'I bet they're doing a video for "Top of the Pops".'

His mother, firmly doling out ham rolls and tuna fish sandwiches, ignored this remark.

'Will you have your tea now, love?' she asked her husband, 'or d'you want a slice of pork pie?'

Without waiting for an answer she poured him some tea from the thermos.

The ticket-collector meanwhile had recovered and got to

his feet, looking distrustfully at the schoolboy as if suspecting him of being responsible for his condition in the first place.

'Are you in charge of this reptile, madam?' he asked Gruesome. 'Do you know it's an offence to travel with a poisonous reptile improperly secured on British Railways?'

'She's not a poisonous reptile,' said Gruesome. 'She's a grass snake. Perfectly harmless.'

'It's Gravella of the Ghouls,' cried the small boy in the Mickey Mouse T-shirt. 'You know . . . "unzipping the zombies . . . *boom* . . . *boom*".'

'Sit down Gary and eat your sandwiches,' said his mother.

Gary took no notice. 'Aren't you?' he persisted to Gruesome. 'Aren't you Gravella?'

At that moment Leotard came through to see if Gruesome needed any help.

'There, you see,' Gary said triumphantly to the ticket-collector. 'That's one of the ghouls.'

'Ghouls or no ghouls,' said the ticket-collector, 'that snake is not properly restrained.'

'It must have crawled through one of the holes in the suitcase.'

The ticket-collector was leafing through a thick book he'd produced from an inner uniform pocket.

'That'll be £6.21 for the snake,' he said.

'What?' said Leotard. 'She's not taking up any space.'

'I should really fine it for attempting to travel without a ticket,' the ticket-collector added, 'never mind assault and breach of the peace, but if you'll just keep it quiet from now on . . .' He looked sternly at Gruesome, and Wriggoletto, from her lofty position, looked beadily back at him.

10

At last they arrived at King's Cross station. When Gruesome, Bloodsocks (in basket), Wriggoletto (neatly plaited in and out of Gruesome's hair), Leotard (with frog basket), two suitcases and assorted carrier bags had managed to disembark, they then had to remove the coffin from the guard's van. Gruesome and Leotard managed to balance it on a trolley and piled all the rest of the luggage on top.

As they made their way out into the main station area, they met with shocked comments:

'Ought to have more respect,' muttered a short, middle-aged woman to her husband.

'Their own mother,' confirmed one railway guard to another. 'Brought back from abroad, you know.'

'Yes. S'fact. Got that . . . what d'you call it . . . lastic fever.'

'Just fancy. Piling all their luggage on top of the coffin like that.'

'Well, I don't expect her inside cares,' said an old man. 'Got more important things to worry about, I reckon.'

Gruesome and Leotard at last persuaded a taxi driver to strap the coffin on top of his luggage rack.

'Your mum is it?' he said to Gruesome. 'Merry as a cricket she'll be on top. There you go.' He bestowed the rest of their luggage (except for Bloodsocks' basket) in the boot.

'Now listen, Grue,' Leotard said when they'd got settled in the taxi. 'We're not going to my Auntie Pat's. She'd have fifty-nine pink fits if she saw all this lot, especially Wriggoletto. Plus she's allergic to frogs.'

'But where are we going then?' asked Gruesome. 'I don't know anyone in London.'

'Ah, but I do,' said Leotard. 'At least our Ron does. He gave me an address. Here it is. A friend of his called Billy lives there. 94 Gorefull Road, Pinkley Green. It's just near the tube but I don't fancy hiking that coffin up and down the escalators.'

The taxi-driver laughed so loudly that Gruesome nearly dropped Bloodsocks.

'I'd like to see that,' he said, zooming abruptly to the left and narrowly missing a 52 bus. 'Just imagine if the old dear (no disrespect darling) fell out. "Corpse found on Victoria line".' He laughed again, even more raucously than before.

'I'll pay for the taxi. Ron gave me some money. I reckon we should start a group, Grue. All those kids on the train thought you were Gravella of the Ghouls.'

'Don't be daft,' said Gruesome crossly. 'I can't sing or play an instrument.'

'So what?'

They eventually drew up at the end of a narrow road. On one side stood a line of khaki-coloured council flats, ugly and uninviting. Opposite was a street of three-storey houses in varying degrees of decay and dilapidation. The windows were curtainless or sported Indian cottons, bath-towels or seersucker tablecloths and the front doors and window-frames had little paint. Broken panes of glass in doors or windows had been roughly jammed with cardboard or plasterboard. The front walls were crumbling. The four feet of front gardens were either full of discarded mattresses, blankets and suitcases or were over-abundantly fertile in vegetation so that twelve-foot-six flowers ran amok and shrubs, hopelessly out of control, lurched towards the pavement.

No 94 had vegetation rather than rubbish, Gruesome noted as she and Leotard started to haul their luggage on to the pavement.

A girl with black spiky hair, black tights and black cape painted with silver stars, and a youth in long johns dyed black and black silver-studded jacket and a black bowler hat passed by.

'There's this amazing play on at the Old Ambulance Station,' said the youth as he stepped over the coffin and the frog basket. 'By Charlotte Bill.'

'Really?' said the girl, stopping to tickle Bloodsocks who had just succeeded in fighting his way out of the dog basket.

Leotard rang the bell.

'It works,' he said.

After a long pause, Gruesome peered at something scratched in the lower left door-panel.

'"Open string",' she read out.

'Oh, right,' said Leotard.

He scrabbled inside the letter-box and came up with a key on a long piece of string.

'Right lad,' said the taxi-driver. 'Just hold the door open and I'll stick the old lady inside. Don't weigh much, do she?' he said to Gruesome.

'Er . . . no,' said Gruesome.

'Cor, she should feel at home here,' he said. The inside of the house had a peculiar musty damp smell rather like rotting teeth and mouldy leaves.

'Phew!' Gruesome flopped down on the floor, too tired for a moment even to look at the rest of the house. 'Tell you what, Leotard. I like the atmosphere here. It smells just like a graveyard.'

'You're right there,' said Leotard. 'I don't reckon this friend of Ron's is here.'

'I wonder if anyone at all lives here,' said Gruesome.

44

11

In fact there were quite a few people living in the house but not Billy, Ron's friend. Only two lived there on a regular basis. Others came and went or spent one day or night a week there, or every other Tuesday, or had similar arrangements. The house was a squat and a lot of people had come, stayed in a room for a while and moved on to something better. At the moment there seemed to be only two occupants. A black girl called Maria lived on the second floor. She was seldom to be seen. She left the house early in the morning Mondays to Fridays and returned late every night except Sunday. When they got to know her they found that she had a cleaning job in some offices in the mornings, then went on to Wimbledon School of Art and had a cleaning job at a hospital in Clapham in the evenings.

The other occupant was Julian. He sold things from suitcases in Oxford Street on Mondays, Thursdays, Fridays and Saturdays and played the violin on the tube on Mondays (Northern line), Tuesdays and Sundays. Wednesdays he generally stayed in bed all day after making a huge potful of soup for all the occupants.

Gruesome took the room on the ground floor so she didn't have to carry the coffin upstairs.

Bloodsocks padded slowly from room to room, sniffing scornfully and lashing his tail in a disgusted manner. Gruesome had no doubt what he thought of his new abode.

The room was quite bare except for a straw mat in the middle of the floor and a much-stained tablecloth pinned up at the window. Several layers of wallpaper were peeling off the walls.

'No one used this room before you,' said Maria, 'so you can do what you like with it.'

Gruesome pinned up her collage and snakeskins.

46

Upstairs, on the first floor, was the kitchen. This had a table, three chairs, a cooker, a fridge, a stone sink and three shelves full of cooking pots and crockery, all left behind by previous squatters.

The sink was stacked high with dirty plates and crockery. A panful of soup, some grated cheese turning mouldy on a plate and one boiled potato with a toothmark in the side lay on the table. A dish of rice with some sliced boiled egg on top stood on the fridge.

'Great,' said Leotard. 'Mum'd have gerbils if she saw this.'

Various notices told other occupants or their friends where they were:

'Ben. See you at Neil's.'

'Afe. Gone to the Ritzy. Bella.'

Another, dated December 1980, said 'Happy Christmas Charlie from Sita' in faded green ink.

Over the next few days Gruesome went to sign on. Nobody stared at her as they had done at first in the DHSS in Trumpington. There were so many people of all different shapes, sizes, colours and conditions that Gruesome's fangs and silver-spotted face passed completely unnoticed. It took her all day going from one place to another.

'You'll not get any giro till we get your file through from Trumpington,' said the last clerk she saw, a bespectacled Indian in a sari. 'It could take up to six weeks.'

'Don't you believe it,' said a woman sitting nearby. 'You'll be lucky if you get anything inside three months.'

She then embarked on a long tale involving a history of lost files, angry letters and phone calls. Gruesome began to edge away, wondering what Bloodsocks was getting up to back at the squat.

'Had to stay here all day in the end,' the woman said triumphantly advancing on Gruesome as she retreated and pinning her against a wall. 'Got here 9 o'clock in the morning and stayed till closing-time.'

Gruesome began to scratch at one of her silver spots. 'I think you'd better move away,' she said desperately. 'I'm afraid I might be infectious.'

The woman suddenly focussed on Gruesome and took note of all the spots.

'What is it?' she said, moving away sharply. 'Did you say it was catching?'

'Acute vampirosis, I'm afraid,' Gruesome said.

The woman took off without another word as if a Social Security snooper were after her.

As Gruesome tried to let herself into Gorefull Road, she found her path blocked by a sofa. It was her very own sofa from Wellington Street. Leotard looked out from a second floor window.

'Hiya Grue,' he shouted. 'Your furniture's come and I've got some great news.'

12

Gruesome climbed over the sofa.

'I can't get in,' she yelled. 'It's blocking the keyhole. Gibbering graveyards! What a place to leave it.'

'Den was in a hurry,' said Leotard. 'The bottom window's open. Get in there.'

Gruesome worked her way through the undergrowth and heaved up the window. A large piece of window frame fell off into the 'garden'. She went through into the long back room. Bloodsocks was chewing an evil-looking fish-head he'd scavenged from the dustbin. Upstairs in the kitchen, Wriggoletto was lying in a perfect figure of eight on top of a dish of rice. A big pot of soup was bubbling away on the cooker – it must be Wednesday.

'Better watch out, Wriggoletto,' she said, 'or you'll end up in the soup.'

Gruesome went on upstairs, up and across from the kitchen. She gave a quick peek in. Julian was lying sprawled on a mattress, his clothes piled in little heaps round the floor. On the next floor was a junk room and across from that, Maria's room. Maria slept in a hammock slung precariously from two staples on opposite walls and her possessions hung in wire baskets suspended from the ceiling, some of which could only be reached by a builder's ladder propped against one wall.

Gruesome went on up to the top floor. Leotard had a mattress on the floor and had stuck hooks all over the walls to hang his clothes on.

A mural of a Caribbean fishing-village painted by a previous occupant covered the walls.

In the bathroom, Marcus had taken up residence along with some photographic equipment, twenty empty milk bottles and half a typewriter.

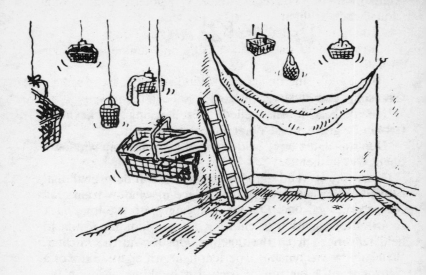

Gruesome sat down on the floor.

'So what's happening?' she asked. 'Looks like I won't get any dole for yonks. Good thing there's no rent to pay.'

'Not to worry,' said Leotard. 'Guess what? I've entered us for a talent contest on Saturday. It's at the Old Midnight Hall Dance Studios. We can win some money and it's £1.00 per contestant to enter.'

'What d'you mean, talent contest?' asked Gruesome.

'You know,' said Leotard. 'Singing, dancing, telling jokes, ventriloquists, tightrope walking – whatever.'

'But what can we do?' asked Gruesome. 'Honestly Leo, you're cracked. I don't know any jokes and I can't walk a tightrope. I don't even think I can fly any more, I'm so out of practice.'

'Mmmmm,' said Leotard. 'We might be able to work that into the act. Now, listen a minute,' he said, as Gruesome started to object. 'I've put us down for a pop group. Those kids on the train gave me the idea. How about the name "Gruesome and the Gravebugs"? You sing and dance, I'll play the guitar and we'll train Bloodsocks to howl at the right moment. You could have Wriggoletto coiled round your head. Brilliant.'

'You're mad,' cried Gruesome. 'We can't do it.'

'Nobody can,' said Leotard. 'It's only amateurs. They're usually terrible.'

'But I can't sing or dance,' said Gruesome. 'And anyway we haven't any instruments. And you can't play the guitar.'

'I can,' said Leotard. 'I've been learning at school. It's dead good.'

'I didn't know that,' said Gruesome in surprise, 'but I still can't sing and dance.'

'Course you can,' said Leotard. 'Maria'll help you. She's into hip hop and break-dancing. Let's see how bendy you are. Spin round on one foot.'

Gruesome twirled.

'Terrific,' said Leotard. 'Now, fall forward on to both hands.' Gruesome did. 'Up again. Down again. Up again. Down again. Up again.'

'That's not dancing,' Gruesome said.

'Great,' said Leotard. 'You're not even panting. You're just like a piece of elastic. Now,' he went on but he stopped as he saw Gruesome had stretched out on the floorboards. 'Get up Grue, we've got work to do. There's a prize of

'£100.00 per performer for the first, you know – something like that.'

Gruesome got up unwillingly.

'Now drop on one hand and spin over.'

Gruesome did this without effort.

'You're a natural,' said Leotard.

'Maybe,' said Gruesome grudgingly, although she was secretly rather pleased. No one had told her she could do anything before. Uncle Batticoop had always said she was good for nothing, especially when he, Four-Fanged Francis (now Three-Fanged Francis), Hideous Hattie, Annelid and Hirudinea had turned her out of Trumpington churchyard.

'But what about instruments?'

'I can borrow a guitar from Auntie Pat,' said Leotard. 'What else do we need? There'll be a piano at the dance studios – p'raps we could rope in Julian or Maria to play it. Then we need some drums.'

Julian, aroused from his mattress, confessed to having had piano lessons for many years.

'But what about my violin?' he asked. 'They like it on the Northern Line. Gives a bit of class to a group. Maria can play the piano. A four-piece band with singer and dancer. Great.'

'I can't sing,' wailed Gruesome.

'Rubbish,' said Julian and Leotard together. 'Anyone can sing.'

'You don't need to.'

'And she can break-dance as well,' said Leotard proudly.

'Fine,' said Julian, combing his straggly beard with a fork. 'So what are we going to sing? And what's the name of the group?'

Maria, when she arrived home on her buttercup yellow bicycle, proved to know someone who had a drum kit in his basement.

'So it's "Gruesome and the Gravebugs",' said Leotard. 'Me, you and Julian are the Gravebugs.'

'But what on earth are we going to sing?' asked Gruesome.

13

The next day Gruesome received a copy of the *Daily Pancake* from Mr Todd.

'FRACAS AT RAILWAY STATION' ran the headlines. She skimmed the article quickly . . . 'London train delayed by unruly vampires . . . vulture in intensive care . . . five vampires answering to the names of Mr B Coop, Miss Anne Lid, Mr F Francis, Miss H Hattie and Mr H I'Rudin were held on charges of assaulting British Railway officials and unlawfully detaining a train. Kept in custody pending further investigation.'

'They won't like it much in prison,' said Gruesome to Leotard. 'Still, I don't see what I can do about it.'

'Be glad they can't come here and worry you for a bit,' he said. 'Doesn't say why they came back from Dieppe, does it?'

'No,' said Gruesome. 'More concerned with the "injuries sustained by BR officials" and "annoyance caused to passengers" blah blah blah . . .'

After midnight, they all assembled in the squat next door where there was an old piano in the cellar.

'I've got the start of a song,' said Leotard. 'What about calling it "The Skeleton Jump"? Listen:

"Down in the graveyard
　　Moan Moan" (Bloodsocks can do that)
"There's a rattle and a groan.
Down in the churchyard
　　Moan Moan.
There's a bumpety bumpety bump.
　　Moan Moan" (Violin sounds)
"It's known as" (Everybody)
"The Skeleton Jump
　　JUMP"

'This is where Gruesome stops singing and does her body-popping routine.'

'Sounds awful,' said Julian.

'Sounds great,' said Maria, simultaneously.

'I can't sing,' wailed Gruesome.

Bloodsocks, who was sitting on top of the piano, began to howl. He was not at all pleased by the way things were developing. The standard of cooking in the squat was certainly not up to what he had come to expect. He had had to roust about looking for his meals which were dumped down anywhere in an old saucepan lid or on an old cracked plate. No one pampered him any more or even noticed where he was most of the time. Gruesome was so delighted with the house – its general atmosphere and smell and the delicately-rotting front garden – that she spent most of her time lying idly flat on her back.

'*Tinkle tinkle*,' went the piano.

'*BONG BONG BONG*,' went the drums.

'*AHiiieeeee*,' went the violin.

'Meeeiiiaaaoooowwwwww,' cried Bloodsocks, putting his paws over his ears.

'Brilliant, Bloodsocks,' cried Leotard. 'Fantastic.' He tickled the cat's chins and gave him a big cuddle.

Gruesome tried to sing as they had told her. She felt very silly. Her voice was very high and squeaky when she sang but she was starting to enjoy the dancing and leaping about, which was easy when you were as thin and flexible as a rubber band.

She was wearing some striped pyjama trousers of Leotard's held up with a red and blue scarf and a silk blouse she'd found in a bag downstairs. Her silver spots were almost gone now.

Maria jumped up and kissed Gruesome on each cheek. Then she kissed Julian. Leotard was too quick for her and hid behind a blue-painted door which was leaning against one wall. It had a withered spider-plant in a pot tied round the door-knob. Maria seized hold of Bloodsocks and stroked him, making passionate kissing noises.

'Magnifique,' she cried. 'Très, très, très bon.'

'Her mother's French,' Julian whispered to Gruesome. 'She's bi-lingual.'

'Does it hurt?' asked Leotard, coming out from behind the door but keeping a wary eye on Maria.

For the next few evenings the cellar resounded to the sound of 'The Skeleton Jump'. Different words, music, costumes were tried. Everyone except Maria lost their tempers. She kept on kissing and hugging everyone within reach at least once.

'You soppypot,' shouted Julian at Leotard when he had knocked over his violin. 'There's nothing between your ears but solid concrete. You're a dimbo-dumbo.'

Leotard showed his bad temper by kicking a hole in the cellar door. Bloodsocks sulked and refused to miaow, purr, spit or even move for several hours. Even Gruesome became affected by the tense atmosphere one evening and rushed out of the cellar back to Number 94.

'Fiddle to Leotard,' she shouted, and hurled all the milk saucepans into the street below.

'Faddle to Julian,' and threw both the frying-pans into the street.

'And feedle to Maria.' Out went the big cooking-pot full of soup into the street.

'Bodgers to Bloodsocks.' Out went the wok and all the saucepan lids.

'To blitheration with all pop groups.' Away went the fish slices and the soup ladle.

After that she felt a lot better. No one else in the street took any notice. They were used to sudden patches of loud noise. No traffic except the odd bicycle or taxi ever passed down the road anyway. After a while she went out and carried back in those pots which were still in reasonable condition.

'You Neanderthal jellypoop,' shrieked Julian. 'You threw away all the soup.'

'Don't worry,' said Gruesome. 'I'll make you a wokful of fresh soup, much better than yours.'

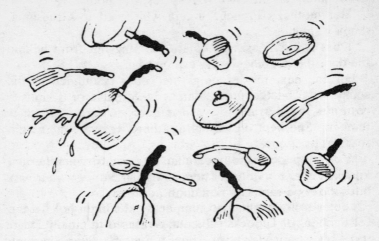

'We haven't got anything to put in it,' said Julian, 'and the off-licence is the only shop round here open at this time.'

'Look there,' laughed Gruesome, pointing to the garden. 'Nettles, dandelions, wild rose, clover and lots more. It'll be out of this world.'

Bloodsocks lashed his tail in rage. Just imagine. A mature cat expected to sustain himself on nettle soup.

14

A few days later the sofa was still outside Number 94 Gorefull Road as no one had bothered to take it in. It had now been pushed back into the path so people could squeeze round it to get through the door, as Gruesome had soon got fed up with people climbing in through the window and disturbing her in the middle of the night. Also, she was afraid of the vampires somehow escaping from prison and creeping in on her just as Hideous Hattie had once done in Trumpington. The sofa proved a pleasant stopping-place for people on their way in or out of the house. People walking down the street sometimes stopped off for a while for a bit of a rest or a sleep.

At last the day of the talent contest arrived. It was Thursday and Julian had taken time off from his Oxford Street stint to take part.

At half past one everyone was assembling at the Old Midnight Hall Dance Studios. It was in the process of being converted into the Midnight Cinema Units 1, 2, 3 and 4 and the audience for the contest, consisting mainly of family and friends of the performers and a large number of people hauled in off the street, was flocking into what was to become Unit 3 since it was the only one with sufficient seats and a suitable performing area.

Rough screens were at the moment separating it from the other units, where painting, plastering and joining were going on at a fairly apathetic rate.

The air was pervaded with the sickly smells of fresh paint, stale kippers and burnt toast. Hammerings and clankings could be heard through the screens. Gruesome and Co. were ushered into a dingy long room walled with mirrors along with all the other performers, who incuded, apart from humans, two poodles and a huge

stuffed polar bear. Bloodsocks had travelled by under-
ground to the studios in his dog box and Gruesome had
not yet let him out. Wriggoletto was concealed inside a red
and black sandbag. Julian was moodily examining his finger
which he had damaged hauling the drum kit up and down
escalators.

'Where's Maria?' asked Leotard.

'There,' said Gruesome, after they had looked all round
and made sure that she was nowhere to be seen, 'I knew we
should never have done this.'

'Cool it,' said Leotard, who was adjusting his black boiler-
suit and the silver cobwebs Julian had tatted for him out of
embroidery silk. All of them except Gruesome had green
and sludge paint for their faces and hands.

Julian was wearing a similar costume to Leotard's but his
boiler-suit was decorated with silver bats made from cooking
foil.

Gruesome was wearing black cotton pyjama bottoms, a
red cotton top and a black sash. They all had black jelly
shoes except for Gruesome who had red ones.

Gruesome let Bloodsocks out of the box. He looked about

60

him with an angry lash of his tail (he'd had no breakfast, unless you counted half a boiled potato). Then he smelt the kippers. His tail fluffed into a question-mark and his whiskers twitched. .

'Where the heckers is Maria?' grumbled Julian. 'She should be here. I left my Oxford Street pitch for this. I'm sure she could skive off art college for a day.'

Just as he said this, Maria arrived. As soon as they saw her, they realized why she was late. Her left arm was in a sling.

'Maria? What happened?' cried Gruesome. 'Can you still play?'

'Oh I'll manage with one hand,' said Maria. 'They'll probably think it's part of the act, man. One of the other cleaners left a broom-handle sticking out, didn't they, and I tripped over it, didn't I? Espèce de cochon.'

'What's that mean?' asked Leotard.

'Don't ask,' said Julian, rolling his eyes in horror. 'You're under-age.'

'Anyway, here I am,' said Maria, enveloping Gruesome and kissing her soundly. Leotard turned to flee but the poodles, the polar bear and a little girl in a pink frilly frock and pink sunbonnet with matching parasol, blocked his way.

But Maria grinned at him and tousled his hair. 'As for you, mon petit chou, wait till you are older.'

No one else escaped her attentions. All the other performers were clasped in her plump arms and kissed soundly, including Bloodsocks, the poodles and the stuffed polar bear. Maria, like the rest of the group, was wearing a tight black boiler-suit which clung to her plump body, and a red silk scarf round her neck, a red butterfly clip perched among her dreadlocks.

An outburst of clapping from the audience told them the show was about to start.

All the performers looked at each other nervously, forgetting any dislike they might have felt in a general fear and distrust of the audience.

'And the first performer today, ladies and gentlemen,'

61

announced the compère, a portly man (dyed black hair, clicking false teeth and a double-breasted navy pin-stripe suit), 'is Miss Sharon Osborne, age 7, who will sing "Animal Crackers in my Soup".'

15

After Sharon Osborne, whose performance induced Leotard to stuff his fingers down his throat and make vomiting noises but which received rapturous applause from a small section of the audience, there was the ventriloquist with the polar bear, who was received in complete silence, a schoolboy comedian, whose jokes were older than he was and a teenage girl who sang 'One Fine Day' from *Madame Butterfly* to a bored but polite audience.

'She's got a good voice,' whispered Gruesome.

'Yes,' said Maria, 'but opera isn't the right thing here.'

After this there was a double act of two girls dressed as clowns. The audience began to laugh.

'They're good,' said Gruesome, who was starting to enjoy it.

'Bet they'd make even your old Uncle Batticoop laugh,' said Leotard.

'Never,' said Gruesome. 'It's said he hasn't laughed since 1764.'

At last it was their turn.

'Ladies and gentlemen,' said the compère, looking at the group with disgust, 'I now present to you the final act in this amazing galaxy of talent . . . Gruesome and the Gravebugs.'

'Come on, Bloodsocks,' urged Gruesome. 'We're on.'

Maria tentatively tried out the piano, Julian tinkered with his violin, Leotard positioned the drum kit and Gruesome cleared her throat. Bloodsocks padded over and sat down beside her. Ah yes, that was definitely a kipper smell. He purred and favoured the audience with a Bloodsocks special smile.

'Gadies and lentlemen,' said Gruesome and there was a sympathetic ripple of amusement. Before this the audience had been not quite sure how to take them, but Gruesome's slip won them over. She didn't risk repeating her mistake but went on. 'Today we are going to sing a song of our own composition entitled "The Skeleton Jump." I am Gruesome Gussie, and these are the Gravebugs – Julian, Maria and Leotard, and this is my cat Bloodsocks. Oh and up here,' she pointed to her head, 'is Wriggoletto.'

There was a brief smattering of applause and then they launched into 'The Skeleton Jump'.

'There's a rattle and a groan
Down in the churchyard . . .'

And Bloodsocks came in, right on cue, with a marvellous howl.

There was a roar of laughter and cheers.

The hammering and thumping which had not assisted some of the other acts stopped entirely. At first workmen were seen peeping through the screen and then, as Gruesome began her body-popping and break-dancing, the screens were pulled aside altogether.

A spontaneous round of applause broke out at Gruesome's dexterity and before long the news, spreading in some way or other out into the street, brought in a number of passers-by.

'Yes man,' they called out. 'That's "The Skeleton Jump".'

The group finished their number to prolonged applause. The local reporter, who had been unwillingly drafted to the talent contest, had reached for his camera, then for his notepad, and then dived for the nearest phone-box.

'Hold it,' he said to the compère. 'Don't let that act go before I get back.'

The compère also could hardly believe his luck. That awful looking bunch of yobs and their revolting cat were obviously going to start a new craze. This could only be good news for the Old Midnight Hall Dance Studios and probably for him. Gruesome was certainly the right name for them.

The applause and the cheering went on for so long after their number that they had to agree to go on playing. Since

that was the only number they knew, they started all over again. Wriggoletto added to the general euphoria by waving her head from side to side when they got to 'Bumpety Bumpety Bump'. Everyone thought she was clockwork. There was no doubt who had won as television reporters, who had been alerted to a new scoop, filmed and interviewed the group.

'Guess what?' said Leotard as at last they were on the way home on the tube. 'They've had to drop someone out of "Top of the Pops" and they're putting us in as a new group instead.'

'Well, that's the last time, man,' said Maria. 'I can't be doing with this kind of ruckus too often.'

'Me neither, man,' said Julian. 'It was fun, but not for all the time.'

And so it was that Mrs Jones, idly flicking the switch of the television set in Trumpington, stopped and stared in amazement.

'Eh, look at this . . . come and look at this. They do have some odd groups these days. Look at that chap on the drums. It looks a bit like our Leotard.'

Mr Jones gave it a quick glance, then a prolonged stare.

'Eh, it is our Leotard. What's he doing dressed up like that? Must be that lummox Ron's doing.'

'Never,' said Mrs Jones. 'Ooh yes, it is him. And there's Gruesome doing that funny dance. Would you credit it? And there's Bloodsocks too. Dunno who the other two are, though. Well. Just imagine. Fancy our Leotard becoming a pop star! He should have told me, though. I might have missed it. I must phone our Pat and see why she didn't tell us.'

She rushed to the telephone to ring up Bet, Ron, her mother, Pat, her friends at work and everyone else she could think of.

'What d'you mean "pop star"?' grunted Mr Jones. 'He's got about as much talent as a bedbug.'

'Well, there you are,' said Mrs Jones happily.

16

During the next few days there was pandemonium at 94 Gorefull Road. The street was crawling with interviewers, reporters and representatives from recording studios. They declared Number 94 delightfully squalid and perched happily on the sofa sipping Perrier water and lemon tea.

'I've had enough of this,' said Leotard, who at last escaped by creeping through a hole in the wall into the next house and out of the back door. 'I'm going off to play Pinball Wizard and tomorrow I'm going home.'

Julian was annoyed too because he couldn't play the violin on the Northern Line any more without being recognized. He had to resort to a disguise. 'I'm moving out,' he told Gruesome. 'There's a really good squat in the next street – this place has got too noisy.' Maria also was not amused. The money had been useful and meant she could give up her cleaning job for a bit, but she didn't want to be interviewed by little magazines and radio stations every five minutes. She also was moving on to another squat. There was some ill-feeling in Gorefull Road generally. No one in the road wanted a spotlight on themselves or their activities.

Gruesome, however, had got an idea. She made several long phone calls to Trumpington.

A couple of nights later she set out to meet the 3 A.M. train into King's Cross Station. There was hardly anyone about except for some people sleeping in cardboard boxes, railway staff and a few passengers. As the train winced to a halt, Gruesome made her way to the reserved carriages. At last she could see Mr Todd alighting from the train and, behind him, the dreaded figures of Uncle Batticoop, Hideous Hattie, Three-Fanged Francis, Annelid and Hirudinea.

'They're feeling very frisky,' said Mr Todd. 'I gave them plenty of steak before we set out and warned them to be on their best behaviour on account of their being let out on bail.'

'Thanks for bringing them down. I'll pay you back all the ticket-money.'

The five vampires rushed towards her. Uncle Batticoop stared for some moments at Gruesome's face, which Leotard had re-painted in shades of purple and acid green before he left. He had also sprayed her hair. Then he looked at the red boiler-suit decorated with silver stars she was wearing.

'Shocking,' he murmured. 'Shocking. To think you were once a respectable vampire from a good churchyard. Where did I go wrong?'

'Respectable vampire,' chimed in Three- (*no*, thought Gruesome) Four-Fanged Francis.

'Hang on,' said Gruesome. 'I thought you lost a fang at the station.'

Four-Fanged Francis beamed triumphantly. 'That's what you thought,' he said. 'Luckily, there's such a thing as SUPERGLUE.'

'Oh,' said Gruesome.

Hideous Hattie, whose hair looked even stringier and more unkempt than usual, spat on the platform and looked at Gruesome in contempt.

'Just look at her hair,' she said. 'Whoever heard of a vampire with orange hair?'

'Disgraceful,' said Annelid and Hirudinea.

'Look,' said Mr Todd. 'Gruesome asked me to bring you down because she thought she could help you, but if you're going to be rude all the time, I shall take you straight back to Trumpington on the next train AND I shall ask them to take you into custody. Then you'll have to go back into prison again. And you know what that's like.'

All the vampires shuddered. 'Never, never, never,' wailed Uncle Batticoop. 'Ah, Gruesome, you don't know what we had to put up with in that shameful place. Two days and nights we spent there. Oh, the misery. No food, no sleep . . .' his voice quavered and Gruesome almost felt sorry for him.

Mr Todd was staying in a hotel and was returning to Trumpington the following day. Gruesome took the vampires in a taxi to 94 Gorefull Road.

She explained to them in the taxi that, yes, it was a house, but it was much better than most. It was old and run-down and decayed and smelt rather like a graveyard. And it was cold and damp. 'That was the worst thing,' shuddered Hideous Hattie. 'Central heating. All the cells were centrally heated.'

All the vampires tutted and hissed in horror.

17

At least the memory of prison made the vampires a little less nasty to Gruesome than usual. Although they quivered with horror as they actually entered the house, the dank musty smell which met their nostrils cheered them a little. 'We can leave the door and windows open if you like,' said Gruesome. 'It won't matter much here. Most of the houses are squats.'

'Toppling tombstones,' erupted Uncle Batticoop as he reached the kitchen and saw Bloodsocks asleep on top of the fridge. 'Can that really be Bloodsocks? He's absolutely BLOATED. Disgusting.'

Bloodsocks wobbled down when he realized who the visitors were. His memories of them were no more pleasant than Gruesome's. He too had often been nipped by Four-Fanged Francis. He stood close to Gruesome, his fur on end, his eyes very sharp and watchful. 'Disgusting,' said Four-Fanged Francis. 'He must be starved into shape. Made to hunt for his food like any other cat.' He fell over suddenly, crashing his head against the table.

'Goodness, you are clumsy,' said Gruesome, laughing as Four-Fanged Francis got angrily to his feet. Uncle Batticoop cuffed him round the head with his top hat.

'Nincompoop,' he boomed. None of the other vampires saw Wriggoletto's tail whisking into a cupboard out of sight.

When Gruesome had shown them all over the house, they all went to sit outside. Gruesome knew she wouldn't get any sleep till daybreak with the vampires around. The vampires sat in the garden among the undergrowth while Gruesome and Bloodsocks sat on the sofa.

'Now,' said Gruesome. 'Tell me why you came back from Dieppe. I thought you had a good job there.'

'Funny people,' sniffed Hideous Hattie. 'They eat frogs on toast.'

'What?' said Gruesome, really shocked. 'How could they?' She thought of Marcus upstairs, happily playing among the photographic equipment in the bath.

Annelid and Hirudinea nodded their heads solemnly. 'Still, what can you expect of humans?' said Annelid.

'Quite,' said Hirudinea. 'French or British, they're all the same.'

'No they're not,' said Gruesome. 'Leotard doesn't eat frogs' legs and nor do any of my friends.'

'Friends,' jeered Hideous Hattie. 'How can you be friends with humans?'

'Anyway,' said Gruesome. 'Surely you didn't leave Dieppe just because of that.'

'Well,' said Hideous Hattie. 'We had to live in a caravan which was terrible and then we were made redundant.'

'Where are Uncle Batticoop and Four-Fanged Francis?' asked Gruesome.

'Oh, they've flown up to the roof for a bit of peace and quiet,' said Hideous Hattie.

'But I need to talk to them,' said Gruesome. 'To all of you together.'

'Well, come on then,' said Hideous Hattie flapping her arms.

Gruesome looked doubtful.

'Surely you haven't forgotten how to fly?' said Hattie. 'That would serve you right. Going to live in a house like that. You pitiful creature.'

Gruesome sighed. She was exhausted. How she longed to crawl in to her lovely comfortable coffin with Bloodsocks on her stomach and Wriggoletto on her head. But first she had to find a job for the other vampires. Otherwise she'd never have a minute's peace. She flapped her arms vigorously and took off.

Goodness, she thought, *I'd forgotten how pleasant it is to fly.* She had a quick fly up and down Gorefull Road before alighting on the roof beside the others. Bloodsocks settled himself more comfortably on the sofa and fell asleep.

Gruesome told them about winning the talent contest and going on the television. She knew they wouldn't approve of it but they might be interested in the money she'd earned.

'I've got some people coming to see you,' she said. 'They might be able to give you a job.'

'What sort of a job?' asked Uncle Batticoop uneasily. He wasn't accustomed to Gruesome taking charge and didn't much like it.

'And where will we live?' asked Four-Fanged Francis. 'Not another caravan I hope.'

'Never,' said Hideous Hattie, tapping her fangs with a loose piece of slate from the roof.

'I'm not sure,' said Gruesome. 'Something to do with films. You can't sing or dance or play the guitar, can you?' Silly question, she thought as soon as she'd asked it. They fell upon her.

'Really Augusta,' began Uncle Batticoop. 'How dare you suggest that any of us would indulge in conduct so unbecoming to a respectable vampire? I'll have you know we come from a long line of highly-respected Transylvanian vampires . . .'

Here we go, thought Gruesome wearily.

'Singing and dancing,' sneered Francis, obviously dying to but not quite bold enough to give her one of his prize nips. He contented himself with flicking a few woodlice at her.

'Playing the guitar,' derided Hideous Hattie.

Annelid and Hirudinea spat down the chimney pot.

Uncle Batticoop took off his top hat and began treading on it, which meant he was getting into a temper. The other vampires shut up quickly.

'You could live here,' said Gruesome. 'It would give you an address and nobody would care if you spent most of the time in the garden. Payment could be arranged in steaks as before.'

'We certainly are not going to sing and dance,' said Uncle Batticoop, '*or* play the guitar.'

'Well, perhaps you wouldn't have to,' said Gruesome. 'They're coming tomorrow at midday.'

'At midday?' wailed Hideous Hattie. 'But you know we'll all be asleep by then.'

'I'll give you blood injections,' said Gruesome. 'That'll keep you awake.'

'That's what we had the other time,' said Four-Fanged Francis. 'You know, at Trumpington Station.'

There was a long silence. No one cared to remember the episode.

'Waaaaaaaaaaaaaa. Aaaaaaaaaaaaaaa. Eeeaaaiieeeeeee-eeeeeeeeeeeeee,' wailed Hideous Hattie lying flat along the roof with one foot trailing in the guttering.

Just as Gruesome was about to ask her what was the matter, there was a loud whooshing sound and a big black shape seemed to fall out of the sky and . . . straight down the chimney.

'Wuneye. Wuneye. My little doodums,' shrieked Hideous Hattie and stepped backwards off the roof.

18

Gruesome blinked a bleary eye at the clock from the safety of her coffin.

What a night it had been! She felt so ill she didn't know if she'd ever be able to get up again.

Trust that stupid vulture to fly straight down the chimney into the attic bedroom. Of course the grate had been boarded up and Gruesome was the one who'd had to climb up the chimney pot and haul Wuneye up again with the help of a coathanger and a piece of rope. If it hadn't been for Wuneye, Hideous Hattie wouldn't have hurt herself falling off the roof on to Bloodsocks who had just leapt down from the sofa to take a stroll. By the time Gruesome had got them apart, poor Bloodsocks had a torn ear and a lump out of his tail and Hideous Hattie had a black eye and bruised arms and legs. The wailings and yowlings and screechings were so bad even the other occupants of Gorefull Road were disturbed and came out to see what was going on.

After she'd seen to them, Gruesome had given Wuneye a thorough wash and then handed him over to Hideous Hattie. As dawn approached she laid all the vampires and Wuneye outside to sleep, some on the sofa and some on the ground. What a night! And now, just when she should be having a lovely sleep, the phone was ringing and she had to get up.

It was Leotard.

'Hi Grue. Guess what? We're not moving after all. There's a terrible scandal here about the ring road. Half the town council's been arrested or something and they're not going to build it. So they won't need to demolish Wellington Street. Mum's hopping mad about it. Says we should get compensation but I don't reckon we will. I'm dead chuffed. I'd much rather stay here.'

'Does that mean I can have my flat back?' asked
Gruesome.

'That's right. Have to go now or Mum'll start rabbiting on
about the phone bill.'

Thank goodness, thought Gruesome. At least I won't
have to put up with this lot much longer. One night of them
is too much. It wasn't worth going back to coffin. Soon,
she'd have to meet the TV people who, because they wanted
Gruesome to do another recording for them, might give the
vampires a job.

Suddenly she realized something was missing. Bloodsocks.
She found him squashed under the cooker. No one could
jump on him there. Gruesome coaxed him out, bathed his
ear and tail and promised him some cream and fishfingers.
Bloodsocks didn't even purr in reply. He felt very low.

Just before twelve she gave the five vampires blood
injections to wake them up. Then they all sat outside, and
waited for the TV men to arrive. At twelve o'clock precisely
a yellow car drew up and two men in denims got out.

They looked at the vampires in amazement. Gruesome
introduced them. 'This is Uncle Batticoop.' Uncle Batticoop
took off his top hat and nodded at them gravely.

'Hideous Hattie.' Hideous Hattie gave them a big grin at which both men retreated nervously.

'Annelid and Hirudinea.' They sniffed.

'And Four-Fanged Francis,' said Gruesome. 'He was Five-Fanged Francis but he lost one in an accident. In fact he lost another the other day . . .' Four-Fanged Francis gave Gruesome a nasty nip.

'Shut up,' he hissed. Gruesome took no notice and told them all about the scene at Trumpington Railway Station.

'Fascinating,' said the tall man.

'Excellent,' said the short man.

They talked for some time and Gruesome explained that the vampires had to work between midnight and dawn and required payment in regular steaks (and extra blood-injections, if necessary).

'That's no problem. Don't worry about that, Miss . . . Viking.'

Gruesome sighed and Bloodsocks rubbed against her leg. He felt things were about to take a turn for the better.

When they'd gone, Gruesome warned the vampires not to get into any trouble with the police because they still had to appear in court.

'I'm not staying,' she told them firmly, remembering what a fuss they'd made when she wouldn't go to Dieppe with them. 'I'm going back to Trumpington.'

'Good,' said all the vampires together, to her great surprise.

'It's so noisy living with you,' explained Annelid and Hirudinea.

Gruesome was so amazed and outraged she nearly bit her tongue off. 'I'll leave most of the furniture. I can always get some more. I'll take my coffin of course and my collage.'

Since Marcus was quite happy where he was, she left him too, and at four o'clock she, Bloodsocks and Wriggoletto set off in a taxi for the station. Bloodsocks crossed his paws that things would go back to normal once they got back to Trumpington and he would live once more on a diet of *Pussiesteaks* and boiled cod.

* * *

79

Some weeks later, happily settled back in Wellington Street, Gruesome was watching the television with Leotard.

'Look,' she cried. 'Just look.'

On the screen Four-Fanged Francis and the other vampires were flying around a room. Four-Fanged Francis crashed clumsily into the wall. A shot of him lying on the floor holding a fang followed. All the other vampires stood round him looking horrified.

'Wait for it,' said Leotard grinning. 'I can guess what's coming.'

There was a loud burst of music and what sounded like a choir of angels sang: 'Don't get in a stew'. Then there was a shot of Four-Fanged Francis being handed a tube. 'Use SUPERGLUE!'

This was followed by a shot of the fang being stuck into place while all the vampires stood round smiling.

'Uncle Batticoop *smiling*,' said Gruesome. 'Now I've seen everything.'